Pia
the Penguin
Fairy

To Nadia Dale, a very special friend
of the fairies!

Special thanks to Sue Mongredien

If you purchased this book without a cover, you should be aware that this book is stolen property. It was reported as "unsold and destroyed" to the publisher, and neither the author nor the publisher has received any payment for this "stripped book."

No part of this work may be reproduced, stored in a retrieval system, or transmitted in any form or by any means, electronic, mechanical, photocopying, recording, or otherwise, without written permission of the publisher. For information regarding permission, write to Rainbow Magic Limited c/o HIT Entertainment, 830 South Greenville Avenue, Allen, TX 75002-3320.

ISBN 978-0-545-27038-0

Copyright © 2010 by Rainbow Magic Limited.

All rights reserved. Published by Scholastic Inc., 557 Broadway, New York, NY 10012, by arrangement with Rainbow Magic Limited.

SCHOLASTIC, LITTLE APPLE, and associated logos are trademarks and/or registered trademarks of Scholastic Inc. RAINBOW MAGIC is a trademark of Rainbow Magic Limited. Reg. U.S. Patent & Trademark Office and other countries. HIT and the HIT logo are trademarks of HIT Entertainment Limited.

12 11 10 9 8 7 6 5   12 13 14 15 16/0

Printed in the U.S.A.   40

This edition first printing, March 2011

Pia

the Penguin
Fairy

by Daisy Meadows

SCHOLASTIC INC.

New York   Toronto   London   Auckland
Sydney   Mexico City   New Delhi   Hong Kong

The
Fairyland
Palace

GALA
FAIRYLAND ROYAL AQUARIUM

Fairyland Royal
Aquarium

Kirsty's Gran's
House

Lighthouse

The Park

Tide pool

Ocean Star Sailing Ship

Lea-On-Sea

Whales

With the magic conch shell at my side,
I'll rule the oceans far and wide!
But my foolish goblins have shattered the shell,
So now I cast my icy spell.

Seven shell fragments, be gone, I say,
To the human world to hide away,
Now the shell is gone, it's plain to see,
The oceans will never have harmony!

Contents

Ice to See You!   1

Let it Snow   13

Ready, Steady, Hatch!   23

Trying Flying   35

A Crystal Cavern   47

Pop-up Penguin   57

Ice to See You!

"*Wheeee!* This is fun!" squealed Kirsty Tate as she sped along on roller skates. "Beat you to that tree, Rachel!"

Kirsty's best friend, Rachel Walker, grinned and picked up speed on her skateboard. "I don't think so," she yelled breathlessly, overtaking Kirsty at the last moment. "I'm the winner!" she cheered, slapping her hand on the trunk of the old oak tree a split-second before Kirsty did.

The two girls laughed. It was a sunny spring day and they were on vacation together at the seaside town of Leamouth. They were staying with Kirsty's gran for a whole week. Today they'd come to Leamouth Park, which was at the top of Leamouth Cliffs, overlooking the sea.

"Doesn't the water look pretty with the sun shining on it?" Kirsty commented dreamily, staring out at the ocean below them. It was a perfect blue. The sun

made thousands of twinkling lights dance on the surface of the water and a breeze gently ruffled the waves.

"I know," Rachel agreed. "It's so sparkly, it almost looks magical." Then she grinned at Kirsty. "Speaking of magic, I hope we meet another Ocean Fairy today!"

"Me, too," Kirsty said. "We're so lucky to be friends with the fairies, aren't we?"

"The luckiest girls in the world," Rachel agreed happily. She and Kirsty had shared lots of fairy adventures

together so far, and at the beginning
of this week, they'd fallen right into
another. This time they'd met the Ocean
Fairies! The girls were helping the
Ocean Fairies look for the seven broken
pieces of their magic golden conch
shell, which kept the ocean world in
order. Each piece of the shell was being
guarded by one of the fairies' animal
helpers, so the hunt was on to find them!

Troublesome Jack Frost had ordered his
goblins to steal the magic conch shell at
the Fairyland Ocean Gala. The clumsy
goblins ended up breaking the shell,
though, which had caused all sorts of
problems throughout the oceans. Now
the broken pieces of shell were scattered
across the seas in the human world. The
girls and their fairy friends were trying

to find them all before the goblins could get their hands on them.

Kirsty and Rachel started down the path again. Before long, Kirsty heard tinkling music drift over to them. "Is that an ice-cream truck?" she asked hopefully, feeling hungry at the thought. Her gran had given them some spending money, and suddenly it seemed like breakfast had been a long time ago.

"Yes!" Rachel said, speeding farther down the path and spotting the colorful van parked near the playground. It was still playing its cheerful tune and a large plastic ice-cream cone rotated on the roof of the van. "Come on, let's go over and have a look."

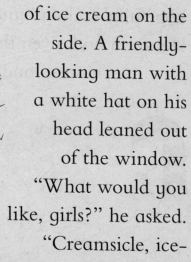

The girls raced up to the van and gazed at the pictures of ice cream on the side. A friendly-looking man with a white hat on his head leaned out of the window. "What would you like, girls?" he asked.

"Creamsicle, ice-cream sandwich, chocolate dipped cone . . . Ooh, how are we going to choose?" Kirsty said, licking her lips as she read. "What are you getting, Rachel?" she asked. When her friend didn't reply, she turned away from the menu. "Rachel?"

Rachel didn't seem interested in the list of ice cream at all. She was staring excitedly up at the roof of the van, where the plastic ice-cream cone was still spinning.

As Kirsty gazed up at it, too, she realized why Rachel was so captivated. Perched on top of the revolving plastic

cone sat a tiny smiling fairy, waving
down at them. It was Pia the Penguin
Fairy!

Pia had coffee-colored
skin and glossy black
hair piled up on her
head and fastened
with a red bow.
She wore a black-
and-white polka-dot
dress with a wide
red belt around the
middle, and red
wedges with black
bows on her feet.

"So, what are you in the mood for?"
the ice-cream man asked the girls.
"Have you decided?"

"Um . . . no," Rachel said, unable

to drag her eyes away from Pia as she fluttered off the plastic cone and hovered in midair like a sparkly butterfly. The tiny fairy gestured for the girls to follow her, and then flew gracefully into a bush behind the ice-cream van. "Actually, I'm not that hungry after all," Rachel said, smiling apologetically at the ice-cream man. "Maybe later. Thanks anyway!"

She grabbed Kirsty's arm and they walked toward the bushes where they'd seen Pia flying.

"Over here!" they heard Pia's silvery

voice call. Kirsty noticed a faint
shimmer in the air above one large
flowering bush.

Kirsty and Rachel made sure that
nobody was looking, then sneaked
behind the large bush. Pia was waiting
for them on a leaf. "Hello again," she
said, smiling at them. "I'm so happy to
see you two.

"I've got a feeling I know where my

little penguin, Scamp, is, and I'm hoping he's guarding a piece of the magic golden conch shell. Will you help me look?"

Kirsty and Rachel didn't need to be asked twice. "Of course!" they said.

A dimple flashed in Pia's cheek as she smiled again. "I was hoping you would say that," she replied, and waved her wand through the air. "Let's go!"

Let it Snow

When Kirsty and Rachel were at the gala in Fairyland, they had learned that each of the Ocean Fairies had a special magical animal helper, who lived in the Royal Aquarium. After Jack Frost made the broken pieces of the conch shell disappear, the Fairy Queen had used her magic to send the magical creatures out into the human world after the shell pieces.

When an Ocean Fairy found her animal again, she would know that a piece of the shell was nearby. So far, the girls had helped Ally the Dolphin Fairy and Amelie the Seal Fairy find their magical creatures along with two pieces of the conch shell. But where would little Scamp the penguin be—and where was the third piece of shell?

There was no time to think about that now though, because fairy magic was streaming from the end of Pia's wand and wrapping Kirsty, Rachel, and Pia in a sparkly whirlwind. It lifted them off the ground and spun them away at a breathtaking speed.

"*Whoaaa!*" Kirsty squeaked. "This is even faster than my skates!"

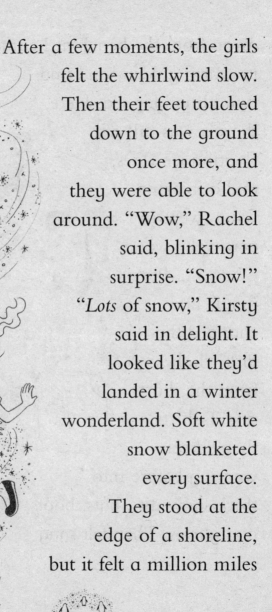

After a few moments, the girls felt the whirlwind slow. Then their feet touched down to the ground once more, and they were able to look around. "Wow," Rachel said, blinking in surprise. "Snow!"

"*Lots* of snow," Kirsty said in delight. It looked like they'd landed in a winter wonderland. Soft white snow blanketed every surface. They stood at the edge of a shoreline, but it felt a million miles

away from the beach at Leamouth, with
its warm golden sand and
twinkling blue sea. Here,
the sea was full of
floating ice floes,
and a freezing
wind swept in
across the water.

Luckily, Pia's
magic had
changed the
girls' clothes
from the shorts
and T-shirts
they'd been
wearing before into
thick snowsuits, hats, boots,
and gloves. They felt snug

and warm, despite the chilly
surroundings.

"Oh, look." Rachel gasped, pointing
ahead. "Polar bears! Aren't
they amazing?"

"Polar bears—ahh, we must
be at the North Pole,
then," Kirsty said,
feeling pleased with
herself for remembering
where the polar bears live.
Pia shook her head,
looking worried. "No,
this is the *South* Pole,"
she said. "Oh, dear. The
polar bears shouldn't be here!
This is all because the golden
conch shell is missing.

Everything's so mixed up in the oceans right now. It's even affected creatures who live *near* the oceans, like the polar bears."

"Well, there are some penguins here at least," Rachel said, pointing to a group of the distinctive black-and-white birds who were huddled together on an icy patch near the water's edge.

"Do you see Scamp with them, Pia?"

Pia flew high into the air and scanned the crowd of birds. "Not from here," she replied. "Let's take a closer look."

The girls and Pia made their way across the snow toward the penguins. As they got closer, Kirsty noticed that some of the taller penguins had something tucked under the feathers above their feet, which they occasionally fussed over with their beaks. "What are they doing?" she asked Pia curiously.

Pia smiled. "They're the dad penguins," she replied. "They're taking care of the eggs by keeping them warm on their feet. It's a very important job."

Rachel watched one proud father penguin

check over his egg with his beak. Unfortunately, he was a little *too* energetic about it. The next thing she knew, the egg had rolled right away from the penguin and was skidding over the slippery ice toward the sea.

"Oh, no!" cried Rachel, breaking into a run. "We've got to catch that egg!"

Ready, Steady, Hatch!

The egg was headed right for the water, and the girls hurried after it as fast as they could. It was so difficult to run on the slippery snow, though! "If only we had our skates and skateboard," Kirsty cried helplessly, skidding on some ice and almost falling over.

"Good thinking," Pia told her, waving her wand. A flurry of blue sparkles streamed from its tip all around the girls. In the next second, a pair of ice skates appeared on Kirsty's feet, and a snowboard under Rachel's.

"That's more like it," Rachel whooped, flying over the snow and catching the egg just before it splashed into the sea.

"Good job, Rachel," Kirsty said, skating over to join her. "And, look, here comes the dad to collect it."

She and Rachel went to meet the father penguin, who was waddling anxiously toward them. "Here you are," Rachel said, carefully setting the egg back on the penguin's big black feet. "No damage done."

But then she heard a faint tapping sound . . . and looked down to see that the egg had cracked right across the middle. "Oh, no!" she cried. "It *is* broken after all."

Pia flew

over and landed lightly on the egg to inspect it. Then she looked up at the girls, her eyes sparkling. "Don't worry," she told them. "That crack is supposed to be there. The chick inside is hatching."

"Oh!" Kirsty cried. "What perfect timing! Now we get to see a newborn baby penguin. How exciting!" Pia laughed at the look of glee on Kirsty's face. "Not so fast," she warned. "It can take the babies a while to break out of their eggs. This one might not hatch for some time."

But just as she was speaking, another longer crack appeared in the egg.

"Come on, little penguin," Rachel said encouragingly, crouching down. "You can do it!"

Tap, tap, tap, went the penguin chick from inside the egg.

"He's chipping away at the shell with his beak," Pia explained, as yet another crack appeared on the surface. This was the biggest one so far. "Actually, I think we might see him any second now. . . ."

Crack! The eggshell broke right in half. There sat a fluffy gray chick about the size of a tennis ball, with soft feet and tiny flippers.

"Oh my goodness." Kirsty gasped, unable to stop smiling. "That is the cutest thing I've ever seen in my life!"

"Totally cute," Pia agreed, as the dad penguin bent down to guide

the baby out of the egg
for his first cuddle. "But
now we really should
be—what's that noise?"

They turned to see
where the sound of
shouting and a roaring
engine was coming
from. A snowmobile
was approaching. Riding on it was
a group of people, all bundled up in
knitted hats and scarves. But they
weren't ordinary people, Rachel
realized. They all had long green
noses. . . .

"Oh, no," she said. "The goblins are
here! They must be looking for a piece
of the conch shell, too."

"They're really upsetting the

penguins," Pia said anxiously, trying to
calm a father penguin. He was looking
very bothered by the noise from the
snowmobile.

The goblins' arrival seemed to have
made the other penguins startled and

jumpy, too. They huddled closer
together to protect their eggs.
Meanwhile, some of the other
penguins waddled away from the
goblins, flapping their flippers
and making snapping sounds
with their beaks.
"What are they doing?"
Kirsty asked Pia, confused.
"It looks like they're trying

to create a diversion," Pia replied. "I think they're hoping to lead the goblins away from the new chick and the eggs." She gasped. "There's Scamp—right at the front of the group. Maybe he knows where the shell is!"

"Follow those penguins!" Rachel cried at once, setting off after them on her snowboard. "If Scamp has found the next piece of the conch shell, then we've got to get to it before those goblins do. Come on!"

Trying Flying

The goblins had also noticed the group of penguins waddling away. Immediately, they turned their snowmobile around so that they could chase after them. "Hey, they're sneaking away!" the girls heard one of the goblins shout eagerly. "Maybe they know something about the missing conch shell. Come on, guys!"

"One of them is very sparkly, too. Look," a second goblin added, narrowing his eyes as he stared. He pointed at Scamp. "I bet he's got something to do with that shell! After them!"

Vrrrooom! went the snowmobile, sending up a shower of snow on each side as it raced along.

The penguins, meanwhile, were moving very strangely. They flapped their flippers and took little hops into the air before landing on their tummies and sliding along the snow.

Rachel looked surprised as she followed them. "Are they trying to fly?" she asked Pia, baffled. "I didn't think penguins could."

Pia, who was perched on Kirsty's shoulder, looked just as confused as Rachel. "They can't *usually* fly," she replied. "But they seem to think they can now! Everything's all mixed up because the golden conch shell is broken." She sighed. "If only the goblins hadn't smashed it before Shannon the Ocean Fairy could play her special song on it, none of these strange things would be happening!"

"Still, the penguins are going pretty fast," Kirsty commented. "They're managing to stay ahead of the goblins at least."

But just then, the goblins surged forward even faster on their snowmobile. One of them leaned out and made a grab for Scamp.

"Oh, no!" Pia cried anxiously. Then she gasped with relief. "Just missed him—thank goodness!"

"Knowing the goblins, they'll definitely try again, though," Rachel said. "We've got to stop them. Let me think. . . ."

Kirsty giggled. "I've got an idea," she said suddenly, as she skated along. "Pia, do you think you'd be able to use your magic to make a big snowman in front of the goblins? It would surprise them, and hopefully make them slow down."

Rachel grinned. "Yes!" she said.

"Maybe the snowman can hold up a warning sign, like crossing guards do near schools? The goblins are so silly, they might even think it's a real person!"

Pia's dimples twinkled in her cheeks as she smiled. "That's a great idea," she agreed. "One crossing guard snowman, coming up!"

She waved her wand, and a stream of blue sparkles flew out of it. A split-second later, a gigantic snowman, glittering with fairy magic, plopped down a short distance in front of the snowmobile. In his hand he held a warning sign.

But instead of saying STOP! CHILDREN CROSSING like a crossing guard's sign, it said STOP! PENGUIN CROSSING! "STOP!" yelled the goblins to the driver, all looking alarmed at the sight. "Whoa!" the goblin driving the snowmobile yelled, swerving to a halt. The penguins continued their funny flying-sliding-waddling across the snow. They were getting farther away by the minute. "Wait a second," one of the goblins said, peering at the snowman. "Why is it all sparkly like that?" He glanced around and then spotted Rachel and Kirsty racing up behind them. "Oh, right. Pesky girls and their fairy friend—*that's* why the snowman is sparkly. They just made it out of magic!"

The goblins stuck out their tongues at the girls and drove around the snowman, continuing their penguin chase. The penguins were now half-sliding and half-flying down a steep slope. Rachel blinked as they suddenly disappeared from view. "Where did they go?" she yelled in alarm, trying to slow down. But the slope was so steep, she found herself going faster and faster. "I can't stop!" she shouted.

"Neither can I!" called Kirsty, who, in her panic, had completely forgotten how to slow down on ice skates. "I think this is the edge of a cliff!" The goblins were shouting, too. "Use the brake! Use the brake!" the ones in the back yelled at the driver. "Stop!"

"Turn sideways!" Pia called to the girls. "Now!"

Rachel and Kirsty turned as hard as they could, and luckily they both managed to skid to a stop just in time, right on the cliff edge. "Phew," Rachel breathed, panting and feeling shaky. "That was close."

The goblins, meanwhile, managed to stop the snowmobile, but the driver braked so sharply, they were flung

right out of it. Now they were tumbling
down the slope, gathering snow as they
went.

"It's a goblin snowball," Kirsty said,
her eyes wide at the sight of the huge
white ball, with green arms and legs
sticking out, all waving furiously. "It's
heading straight for us!"

"They're going to knock
us over the cliff!"
cried Rachel.

A Crystal Cavern

Quick as a flash, Pia waved her wand.
Sparkling fairy dust billowed around
the girls. Then, just as the goblins were
about to crash into them, Kirsty and
Rachel felt themselves shrinking smaller
and smaller. Wings sprouted on their
backs. They were fairies again!

The goblins tumbled right off
the cliff. But the three fairies
fluttered up, just in the nick
of time! "Phew,"
gasped Kirsty,
her heart thumping
at their close escape.
"Thank you, Pia."

Pia was
busily waving
her wand
again, though.
"As much as
those goblins
annoy me, I'd better
give them a soft
landing," she explained. The girls saw a
huge drift of soft powdery snow appear
beneath the falling goblins.

Plop! Splat! Thump!

The goblins dropped into the snowdrift and sank. Snow flew everywhere as they scrambled to get out. Their arms and legs waved wildly!

"Let's let them figure it out and fly after the penguins," Rachel suggested. "I can't see them anywhere now, can you two?"

"No," Pia said, looking around. "Let's swoop down low. We might be able to pick up their trail."

The three friends soared over the cliff,

their hair streaming in
the wind as they
flew.

Once they were closer to the ground,
Kirsty spotted some distinctive penguin
footprints.

"They're heading that way!" she
called, pointing ahead. "Come on, let's
follow them."

At first, the footprints seemed to lead
straight into an icy wall. But as the
fairies flew nearer, they realized that the
wall was actually the entrance to an icy
cavern.

The big snow-covered archway that
led to the cavern was almost invisible
against the pure white landscape.

"Ugh, my feet are so
cold and wet," Rachel
heard the goblins
grumbling behind
them. She quickly
turned and saw
that they had
all managed
to climb out
of the snowdrift.
They were looking very grumpy.

"Quick, let's fly inside the cave," she
said in a low voice, not wanting the
goblins to notice them.

Pia and Kirsty agreed, and they
all darted into the gleaming cavern.

Glittering icicles hung from its roof.
The walls and ground were covered in
thousands of twinkling ice crystals.

"There's Scamp!" Pia cried in delight,
flying over to a cute little penguin
who was standing in the middle of the
cavern.

He squeaked excitedly as he
saw her. He waddled
over at once and
gestured at the
ceiling with one
of his flippers.

"There it is,"
Rachel exclaimed,
gazing up and
beaming as she
saw the sparkles
shining from the

ceiling. "The shell piece has been frozen into one of the icicles!"

"Oh, clever Scamp," Pia said, planting a fairy kiss on his head. "Good job! Now, how are we going to get this down?"

She, Rachel, and Kirsty flew up for a closer look at the shell-icicle. But before they could say another word, they heard stomping footsteps . . . and in came the goblins.

"Aha! Fairies!" one of them said, spotting Pia and the girls. "What's that they've found up there?"

"Ooh! Ooh! It's a piece of that magic shell!" a second goblin yelled.

The goblins cheered. "Let's use snowballs to get it down!" one of them suggested. He scooped up a big handful of snow and packed it into a tight round snowball.

Splat! Splat! Splat! The goblins all copied their friend, throwing snowball after snowball at the icicle.

Kirsty, Rachel, and Pia had to dodge out of the way as the icy snowballs flew at them. "Hey!" Pia yelled. "Be careful! You don't want to break it!"

But the words had only just left her mouth when—*smash!* The icicle shattered and the shell piece went flying.

"Get it!" shouted the goblins.

"Get it!" cried the girls.

Pop-up Penguin

Luckily, the piece of shell landed near Scamp. He picked it up and tucked it under the fluffy feathers above his feet, just like Kirsty and Rachel had seen the dad penguins do to protect their eggs. The goblins lunged toward Scamp, but when the other penguins saw what was happening, they huddled around Scamp to protect him.

"Out of the way, penguins," one of the goblins grumbled, trying to push through them. He didn't make it very far, getting a few sharp jabs from the penguins' beaks for his rudeness.

"*Ow!* Stop pecking me! *Ow!*" he cried, rubbing his arm. The other goblins were

also being pecked by the penguins. They were determined to keep their new friend Scamp safe.

"Where *is* Scamp?" Kirsty whispered from where she, Rachel, and Pia were hovering above the black-and-white birds.

Before Pia could answer, Scamp's head popped up from the penguin huddle. He squawked, teasing the goblins.

"Grab him!" one of the goblins yelled angrily, still trying to push through the penguin crowd.

But moments later, Scamp popped up from a different part of the huddle and gave another playful squawk.

Pia giggled. "He's really having fun with those goblins, isn't he?" she said. "But maybe I should get him out of there now."

Scamp popped up again and one of the goblins made a lunge for him. He was just about to grab ahold of the little penguin when Pia quickly waved her wand, making Scamp and the shell fairy-size. Then, she flew in to snatch them up herself. The goblins grabbed wildly for Pia, but she managed to fly high enough that she was out of their reach.

"Let's get out of

here," Rachel said. The three fairies zoomed out of the cavern, with Pia holding Scamp and the shell piece close to her.

"We did it!" Pia cheered, cuddling Scamp tightly. "Well done, girls. Another piece of shell is safe—that's wonderful news."

"Not so wonderful for the goblins," Kirsty said. They trudged out of the cavern below, looking very gloomy, and bickering about who was going to tell Jack Frost the bad news.

"No," Rachel agreed.

"But the penguins seem happy. And look, they've stopped doing that strange trying-to-fly thing now."

Pia smiled as the penguins trooped out and waddled along the ice back to the sea. Once in the water, they began swimming and diving just like normal.

"I think it must be because we've found another piece of the shell," she said. "Little by little, the ocean is returning to how it should be. Hooray!" She stroked Scamp's glossy feathers. "Now we should get the shell piece back to the

Royal Aquarium in Fairyland, where
it will be safe. Thanks for everything,
girls!"

"Thank *you*," Kirsty said, hugging her.
"That was fun!"

"Bye, Pia, bye, Scamp," Rachel said.
"I loved seeing all the penguins—

especially that little baby. So cute!"

Pia waved her wand and a flood of
fairy dust streamed around
Kirsty and Rachel.
Instantly, they were
spun into the air by a
glittery magic
whirlwind. Moments
later, they found
themselves back in
Leamouth Park.
They were regular
girls again, back in
their summery
clothes, complete
with their roller skates
and skateboard.

One thing was different, though—they were each holding a huge ice-cream cone, filled with pink and white scoops of ice cream and covered in sparkles! "Yum!" Kirsty said in delight, taking a big bite of hers. "Delicious!" Rachel grinned and tried hers, too. "Tastes like magic to me," she said. "What an *ice* way to finish an adventure!"

Pia the Penguin Fairy has found her piece
of the golden conch shell!
Now Rachel and Kirsty must help

Tess
the Sea Turtle Fairy!

Join their next underwater adventure
in this special sneak peek. . . .

A Magic Sandcastle

"Should we build another tower, Kirsty?" Rachel Walker asked her best friend, Kirsty Tate.

The two girls were kneeling on the beach making an enormous sandcastle. They'd been working on it all day in the sunshine. The castle had turrets and towers and archways.

"Oh, yes, what a great idea!" Kirsty said with a grin. She picked up her bucket. "Let's start decorating the castle, too. We can use those pretty pink and white shells we found earlier."

Carefully, Rachel began to build the tower. Kirsty tipped the shells out of her bucket and began sorting through them.

"Look, Kirsty, the sun's starting to set," Rachel pointed out, noticing that people were packing up and leaving the beach. "We'll have to go back to your gran's soon." The girls were spending their spring vacation in Leamouth with Kirsty's gran.

Kirsty's face fell. "I know we've had a great time on the beach, Rachel," she sighed, "but we haven't seen even a *single* magical fairy sparkle all day! I was hoping we were going to find another missing piece of the magic golden conch shell."

"Me, too," Rachel agreed. "But don't forget what Queen Titania always says—we *have* to wait for the magic to come to us!"

"It doesn't look like any magic is going to come to us today, though," Kirsty remarked. She began pressing rows of tiny, creamy shells onto the sides of the sandcastle.

"Isn't our castle great, Rachel?" Kirsty said proudly, sitting back on her heels to take a look. There was hardly anyone left on the beach now except for the two girls.

Rachel nodded. "It looks a bit like the Fairyland Palace with all those towers," she replied. "Except our castle isn't so sparkly, of course!"

Suddenly Kirsty gave an excited cry. "Are you *sure*, Rachel?" she asked with a big smile. "Look in there, under that archway!"

Rachel bent forward on her hands and knees and peered inside the sandcastle. Then she saw it! A glittering, golden light was shining right in the very center of the castle.

"Kirsty, I think it's a fairy!" Rachel gasped as she spotted a tiny figure dancing gracefully through the sandy rooms. "It's Tess the Sea Turtle Fairy!"